For the past staff of the SJS Bug Hotel ~ S S

For my dad, I love you ~ L M

LITTLE TIGER PRESS LTD,
an imprint of the Little Tiger Group
1 Coda Studios, 189 Munster Road, London SW6 6AW
Imported into the EEA by Penguin Random House Ireland,
Morrison Chambers, 32 Nassau Street, Dublin D02 YH68
www.littletiger.co.uk

First published in Great Britain 2022

FSC
www.fsc.org
MIX
Paper from
responsible sources
FSC® C017606

The Forest Stewardship Council® (FSC®) is an international,
non-governmental organisation dedicated to promoting responsible
management of the world's forests. FSC® operates a system of forest
certification and product labelling that allows consumers to identify
wood and wood-based products from well-managed forests.

For more information about the FSC®, please visit their website at www.fsc.org

THE HOTEL FOR BUGS

Suzy Senior   **Leire Martín**

LITTLE TIGER

LONDON

A buzz of excitement hung over the square.
The band played a fanfare, balloons filled the air.
The manager threw the grand doors open wide,
"I'm pleased to announce

WE ARE OPEN!"
she cried.

HOTEL

The crowd started clapping and then with an **"OOOH!"**
They peeked through the entrance to get the first view
Of huge, **BOUNCY** sofas and soft, **MOSSY** rugs
In the brand new and fabulous **HOTEL FOR BUGS!**

They **swarmed** up the steps
and they **poured** through the door.
They **flocked** round the lanterns
and nibbled the floor.

They buzzed round the
buffet, then finally
"Ahh . . ."

. . . They spotted the pool and the *fancy* new spa!

They checked out the Larva Club –
open **ALL** day,
With loads of fun games
for the young ones to play.

LARVA
CLUB

The bugs were on holiday!
Time to **relax!**
But then something made them
all stop in their tracks . . .

Someone slid in through the new hotel lobby,
Somebody **squishy**
and **shiny**
and **BLOBBY**.

A thin trail of **SLIME** glittered bright in the gloom.
"Hello," said the slug,
"may I please book a room?"

The manager **TWITCHED** her antennae in **fright**.
"I'm sorry," she said. "But we're **full** for the night.

And well – if you notice – this hotel's for **BUGS**.
Our guests won't expect to be sharing with **SLUGS!**"

The slug looked **BEWILDERED.**
He said, "Are you *sure*?
That's **REALLY** unfair!"
Then he slid out the door.

"Oh, **phew!**" said the manager,
wiping her brow.
"Don't worry, he's *gone*.
Things are fine again now."

The insects all stared,
then they nodded, unsure.
They looked at the pathway
of **SLIME** out the door.

Then, suddenly, one of
the tiny young bugs
Stepped up and demanded,
"Hey, **what's** wrong
with **SLUGS?**"

"So maybe they're **SLIMY**
and haven't got wings,
Or legs, or antennae,
or well, lots of things.

But honestly, have a
good look at us bugs;
We're ALL pretty **ODD!**
We're much *weirder* than
SLUGS!

Like **me**," she suggested,
"with ears on my knees!

And Horsefly's a **VAMPIRE**,
and so are the fleas."

The dung beetle nodded,
"I roll balls of **poo**."

And Woodlouse admitted,
"My **blood** is pale blue."

The spider said,
"I can make thread from my **bum**.
And afterwards, sometimes
I *eat* the stuff!
Yum."

Then Butterfly added,
"I taste with my **FEET**.
I stomp on the flowers
to see if they're **sweet!**"

The **STINK** bug just grinned
and said nothing at all . . .

And soon a **FOUL SMELL**
filled the whole of the hall.

"You see?" coughed the bug.
"Being different is
COOL!"

The manager nodded.
She felt such a *fool*.

"Perhaps," said a fly, "we should ALL go away.
It doesn't seem right that *we BUGS* get to stay!"

A few grabbed their luggage, all ready to go.
The manager *blushed*, shook her head and said,

"No!

If **ANYONE** ought to get moving, it's **ME.**
I've been *so* unkind, and I just didn't see!
I hope I can fix it. **Please,** just take a seat."
She flew out the door
and shot off down the street.

Then five minutes later,
the creatures all **CHEERED**,
As **Slug** and the manager
both *reappeared!*

"I TRULY am **sorry**,"
the manager said.
"I'll find you a room
with a *four-poster bed!*

Or maybe a suite
with a beautiful view,

A really **posh bathtub**
and **balcony** too?"

"That sounds very nice!"
said the **slug** with a *grin*,
And then he was off
to get all settled in.

That evening, the **slug** and the BUGS couldn't wait
To all get together and *party* 'til late!
They sang karaoke and danced in the hall
Of the brand new and fabulous

HOTEL FOR ALL!